VOLUME ONE

SHORT BITS

FOUR ORIGINAL SCIENCE FICTION & FANTASY STORIES

BELINDA CRAWFORD

HENDRIX & FAUST
PUBLISHERS

Published by Hendrix & Faust, Publishers in 2022
Text copyright © Belinda Crawford 2022

This is a work of fiction. Names, characters, businesses, places, events, locales, and incidents are either the products of the author's imagination or used in a fictitious manner. Any resemblance to actual persons, living or dead, or actual events is purely coincidental.

www.belindacrawford.com

ISBN: 978-0-6450459-3-2 (ebook)
ISBN: 978-0-6450459-4-9 (paperback)

A catalogue record for this book is available from the National Library of Australia

*To Kris,
thanks for the
fabulous title.*

Books by Belinda Crawford

The Hero Rebellion
(Hunter)
Hero
(Race)
Riven
Regan

The Echo
Cold Between Stars
Dark Between Oceans
Echo Between Worlds
(Brother)

Collections
Short Bits Volume 1

CONTENTS

INTRODUCTION

It is a truth universally acknowledged that I suck at writing short stories; it's not that the stories are bad, it's just that I don't really do *short* fiction. Every tale I write, long or short, grows beyond the words that contain it, developing ideas that begged to be followed here and there and everywhere. More often than not, what I intend to be a shorty ends up being the first bit of *something else*.

Sometimes, I'm lucky and enough of the story ties itself off to make a cohesive whole, with beginning, middle and end but sometimes... Sometimes they don't. Sometimes I have a beginning and middle but the end gets lost in a messy "ohhh, I *like* that idea" explosion that eventually leads to a book. Or a series, or a series of series.

Short Bits is a collection of these messy explosions, as well as a few stories with actual, proper endings. They're written for the fun of it, and for practice (I'm going to *crack* that short story nut!), and they're published here because otherwise they're going to sit in a drawer and wait for a day when I *might* get around to turning them into a complete novel (or series, or series of series), and what's the point of that?

If you read a story in here you like and you just *have* to have more, let me know. I'm going to be keeping an unofficial count, and the more people who want a story to continue, the higher it'll move up my never-ending list of "ohhh, I *like* that!", and may, eventually, get turned into a full-fledged book.

Happy reading,

Belinda

REPRISAL

A TALE OF THE LIGHT

INTRODUCTION

Quite a while ago now, I was watching a terrible teen movie about a bunch of high school dudes with magic. It's only redeeming features where the eye-candy and a rather chauvinist plot device where only men could wield magic.

Now, that last part isn't normally a good thing, but in this respect, it ticked me off so much that I came up with the idea for Tales of the Light. If you want to know more about it, check out the *Short Bits* audio commentary (link below) where I take you behind the scenes of each of the stories in volume one.

For now, I won't tell you any more about it, except that *Reprisal* is the prologue of a longer story.

Although it's not my on writing calendar just yet, Tales of the Light is definitely a project I'm keen to get back to.

Scan the QR code for the audio commentary.

Reprisal *was first published as 'Lex Talionis' in 2012 in* Andromeda Spaceways Inflight Magazine *issue 54.*

REPRISAL

The mare's leg is laid open to the bone. Her skin and sinew separated in one jagged stroke from shoulder to knee. She stands lopsided on the other three, sinking into the stall's carpet of straw, her head drooping and her ears wilted. I lay one hand on her nose, gently stroking the white blaze, her lead in my other hand.

Jack is crouched by the wound, his hands bloody. There is an edgy tension in my limbs as my husband's mouth thins and his brow furrows like the freshly tilled fields. He shakes his head. My heart sinks.

He puts his hands to his knees and pushes himself upward. 'She'll have to be put down.'

I stroke the mare's nose. She is a faithful creature, placid with age and years of hard labour. Without her, the fields would not be tilled nor grain taken to the village market. 'We can't afford another horse.

'We'll make do.' Jack looks past me, toward the open barn door. 'I can hitch Daisy to the plough.'

I follow his gaze. The cow awaits her morning milking, lazily swatting flies, untroubled by my son's clumsy pets of her broad shoulder. Her honey-coloured coat is again glossy and her udder full after the lean months of winter but unlike our neighbour's oxen, she is small and delicate.

I turn back, raising my eyes to Jack's. 'There's another way.'

Jack's shoulders tense and the centres of his eyes grow large till only a thin line of blue rings the black. He stares at me for several long seconds and I smile softly, willing him to agree. The Reverend's sermons, full of shaken fists and dire warnings, have frightened us all, inviting suspicion into the village. Our friends and neighbours peer from around their curtains and hold themselves ready to point and cry alarm at the slightest hint of devilry, but there is little choice. We need the mare.

Finally, Jack shakes his head. 'It's too dangerous. If the Reverend should find out...'

'There's no one here to carry tales.' I widen my smile, gesturing around the barn, empty except for us, the horse, and little Devon petting the cow.

His lips tighten. For a moment, I fear he will refuse and wonder what I will do if he does.

Jack nods but his expression remains grim as he holds out his hand for the lead. I place it in his palm and step around him to the mare's shoulder, touching it lightly just above the wound. The unmarred skin is warm and smooth, her chestnut coat silky beneath my fingers and for a moment I stand there, the dusty scent of horse strong in my nose.

I crouch and place my other hand on the mare's knee, a bare inch below the ragged tear. Here, her coat is tacky with blood as it seeps from the wound and an iron tang mixes with her dusty scent.

I close my eyes. A few moments of concentration as I summon the coil of warmth that lives in my belly. It shivers and then leaps to my will, flooding through my chest in a rush that lightens my head.

I take a breath, quieting the magick before drawing it through my hands and sending it into the animal's flesh. The warmth twists and turns, wrapping itself around veins and muscles, pulling them together. It is not enough though, the injury is too great and my power too small, so I steel myself and reach down through my feet and into the earth, seeking more. It comes quickly, flowing hot and rich, burning its way through my hands and into the horse. Behind my lids I can see skin knit together, unblemished and whole, and my head spins.

My eyes open and I smile, barely noticing the grass at my feet, brown and dry, its life taken for the mare.

There is a gasp from behind me. I turn. Euphoria vanishes.

Little Devon stands at the stall's gate, jumping and waving, and next to him – Oh Dear Lord – next to him in her heavy black skirts is Hetty Jones, the storekeeper's wife, a hand over her mouth and a covered basket hanging from the crook of her arm. Her wide brown eyes stare at me with such fear that I think my heart may stop.

Beside me Jack moves, taking a step forward, his face as pale as mine. Hetty's eyes snap from me to Jack, to his outstretched hand. She stares at it like she would a snake, or the Devil himself. She draws back, her eyes growing wider.

'Hetty,' Jacks says and takes another step forward.

The basket falls to the ground, a crock of honey spilling from under the white covering.

Hetty runs.

☾

I stumble in the dark and my heart leaps before I recover my footing.

I pause, clutching little Devon closer, terrified of dropping his precious weight and just as terrified of the stillness of his form. I squeeze my eyes shut and send a prayer to God that my magick wasn't too much.

The mob had come so fast, so much faster than we had thought. Hetty's feet must have flown her to the Reverend. There had been no time to pack the cart, less to hitch it to the mare and take ourselves to safety. Only my magick had allowed our escape, allowed us to slip past the storekeeper waiting at our back door with a torch.

There had been so much confusion, so much fear, and the mare had taken all of my magick to heal. I had reached past the empty tangle of power in my belly, reached once more for the earth when little Devon had clutched at my leg. Thick and rich the power poured through me, igniting the spell on my lips and wrapping confusion around the storekeeper's eyes. My son sank to the ground at my feet, his face pale, a small part of his life absorbed by the spell.

For several moments I stood horrified, looking down at my son's crumpled form. Then Jack yelled at me to run and I scooped little Devon into my arms, feeling his heart beat against my chest, and fled, dashing past the storekeeper's sightless eyes.

Now the breeze at my back brings the whiff of burning wood and my heart leaps. I glance over my shoulder and see the vague glow of the mob's torches over the rise. They are gaining on me.

A faint noise escapes my lips as I look frantically toward the tree line. I have to reach it before they top the rise or all is lost.

Jack is already gone, taken by the mob. I heard our front door splintering as I ran, and knew my husband was not running behind us as he had promised. I dashed through darkness toward the barn, Devon still clutched close, his arms and legs dangling limp by my sides. I reached its dense shadow and turned. The mob had surrounded our house, lighting the night with fire, the Reverend at their head.

People spilled from the front door and my heart clenched when I saw Jack struggling in their midst. They jerked to a halt before the Reverend. The old man leaned forward. Jack screamed. I wanted to scream with him and bit my lip till it bled. I saw Jack crumple, disappearing behind a curtain of bodies. The Reverend shouted and raised something that glinted in the torchlight. I didn't see him bring it down, instead I turned and ran. From behind me Jack screamed again.

The field is soft and my feet sink and slide in the furrowed earth. I cross the field as fast as my sodden skirts allow. My breath comes in rasps and the faint taste of blood coats the back of my throat. My limbs are tired and Devon is heavy in my arms, but the knowledge of the mob at my back and the memory of Jack's horrifying screams keep me moving.

Faster, faster until I fear tripping over my own feet. Twice I risk a look over my shoulder and each time the glow over the rise is brighter. The tree line is close but not close enough. My heart pounds in my ears, louder and louder as I run. It's not loud enough to drown the sudden braying of the hounds.

Oh my Lord, let me reach the trees before they see me.

Only a dozen yards before I'm safe and again I glance over my shoulder. My blood freezes and my feet with it. A silhouette, torch in hand, stands against the sky.

Instinctually, I clutch Devon tighter.

They've found me, oh dear Lord in Heaven, they've found me!

A movement from the figure on the rise sends liquid fire through my veins and I start to run.

I hear a shout and fear lends speed to my feet but the short distance to the trees still seems like a mile.

☾

I crouch lower in the hollow of the firs as the mob draws near.

The dogs run in circles, my magick has confused our trail, leaving them no scent to follow. I squeeze my eyes shut as the glow of the torches approaches.

If they see us, it is over. They will hang me just for being born, and my son... I clutch Devon closer feeling him breathe, warm against my neck.

Oh Merciful Lord, please protect my son from what I must do.

They can't see us, they can't see us.

Behind my eyes Devon blazes with life, so much closer and so much brighter than the earth and roots below. I grit my teeth, fighting an unholy instinct to draw on Devon for my spell, and touch the earth instead, feeling the pull in my belly as the magick comes. It wraps itself around our place of refuge, twisting and turning around the hollowed-out trunk, playing tricks with the moonlight until we're obscured from sight.

They can't see us, they can't see us.

I rock as I repeat my chant, my eyes closed tight against the sight of the mob milling in confusion like their dogs. Soon the chant is all I can hear, all I will allow myself to hear.

They can't see us, they can't see us.

Somewhere in the distance I am aware of the Reverend's voice. It reverberates against the trees and for a moment I am back in the small church, sitting on the hard pew as he stands at the pulpit. Standing as straight as his stooped shoulders will allow, his knuckles white, the wrath of the Lord on his face and promises of damnation on his tongue.

'She's bewitched your dogs, Johnson, you can't deny her perfidy now!'

I squeeze my eyes tighter and think harder to drown the sound of his hated voice.

'... confounded the dogs...'

'She can't go far...'

☽

Dawn breaks before I let the magick fade.

We are alone now. Above me a bird sings in the morning and I look up, spying the white spotted breast and cinnamon wings of a thrush. From somewhere comes the furtive rustling of leaves and something soft and round catches my eye. A hare hops an arm's length from our refuge, its brown sides quivering as it sniffs the air. Its ears twitch once, twice, before it drops its head and paws at the litter of leaves and grass.

For the moment we are safe.

I look down at my son. His soft blonde head rests against my chest. Warm relief twists through me and I press my lips to his curls before resting my cheek against the top of his head and hugging him close.

'Devon,' I say. The hare's long ears twitch at the sound of my voice. My son does not respond. 'Devon.' I look down, noting his pale cheeks and the darkness under his eyes. My heart clutches, something nameless and terrifying crawls into my throat.

My hand shakes as I lay it against his cheek. It is cold. Too, too cold.

'Devon?' My voice rises, becoming strident. The hare lifts its head, ears alert.

I tilt my son's head. It lolls against my arm. His face is lax, without expression, his lips blue. I press my fingers into the juncture between head and neck.

Oh Dear Lord, please, please, please.

☾

I leave my son in a cold grave under the branches of a sapling pine. It will grow. I have ensured that no blade will leave a mark on its smooth trunk. The hare and a nest of starlings paid the price for my spell.

I am cold inside, my innards are laid out next to my son and there is nothing left in me to feel. The coldness is its own comfort though, has its own voice, its own urgings.

☾

The village square is grey, silent, tomorrow giving way to today on the crow of the cock. I stand beneath the oak at its centre, no longer cold, no longer empty. A day and night have passed since I left Devon under the pine and I have used the time well.

Now, this morning under the oak, I wait for the villagers to wake and discover the things I have taken during the night.

A shutter clatters. A candle flickers in the general store.

My breath shortens and my shoulders tighten.

The wind rustles in the leaves above me and from somewhere distant a cow lows. Closer, I hear birds flutter and call. Of the villagers I hear nothing and my chest pounds and squeezes. I take a step forward, then another, willing, hoping, waiting.

It rings out, high and piercing and piteous, a wail from the little house behind the store, full of pain and grief. The storekeeper's daughter has found her parents, cold and still like my little Devon.

I smile and wait for the others.

LITTLE BLACK BOOK

INTRODUCTION

This story is weird. It's one of those little bits of daydream fluff that came out of nowhere and doesn't really *fit* into anything. I'm not even sure I like it that much, but then, I say that about a lot of the stuff I write, particularly after I've just written it. You'll have to let me know what you think.

If you want to hear more, including behind-the-scenes tidbits from the writing of *Little Black Book*, check out the *Short Bits Volume 1* audio commentary.

Scan the QR code for the audio commentary.

LITTLE BLACK BOOK

The little black book was old and tattered, the pages yellowed, edges crumbled – eaten by the rats and other bibliophilic vermin that had infested her aunt's attic.

Not anymore though, not after the fire.

Niyha turned the book over in her hands and wondered if her aunt had done the same, had ever sat in the little hothouse out back and just stared at the faded leather, run her fingers over the words carved into the surface.

"Prina Kolaeda."

Prina Kolaeda. The name sent a shiver down her spine, or maybe that was just the way the letters seemed to writhe. The plain block print stamped into the leather – the faintest hint of gold still clinging to the corners – shouldn't be able to twist around itself and wind around her fingers, but it did. The "P" slipping up over her knuckle, the tail on that final "a" reaching out to entangle her thumb as if to suck her into the journal too.

She shook the letters off and forced herself to put the book down. It was harder than it should have been, her fingers cramped, muscles pulling, tendons standing on end as a little voice in the back of her head screamed at her to hold tight. It was deep and commanding, a hook reaching down into the pit of her, trying to rip her soul out through her mouth.

Niyha breathed – in through the nose, out through the mouth – and concentrated on the cry of the crows in the trees, the sigh of the soot-laden breeze, the distant rumble of cars. She breathed again – in, out – and built a wall between herself and the voice, tall and thick. It screamed one last time, a desperate lunge for the small gap at the top of the wall then died.

Her fingers relaxed, and the book plopped into the garden bed, sinking into the old soil – more dust than loam now and covered in a fine layer of ash.

'Are you happy?' The voice spoke from behind, twisting out of the dead arms of her aunt's wisteria, branches that had once been full of green, now little more than decaying twigs.

'Are you?' she whispered back.

Corrian moved out of the dark. Tall and slim, with hard face almost as ancient as the stones beneath Niyha's sandals, even if age had forgotten to carve the matching lines into his skin. 'Yes,' he said. 'I am.'

Niyha nodded, gaze lifting from the book to the house. The fire had razed it to the ground but had left the fireplaces with their chimneys standing – three silent, blackened sentinels marking the boundaries of the old house.

She wouldn't miss it, wouldn't miss the way the veranda creaked, giving away her every attempt to escape, nor how the old weatherboard siding with its faded yellow paint had shoved splinters under her fingernails. But she would remember them more fondly than she would the shrill screech of her aunt's parrot and the sharp slap of the old woman's hand.

Niyha rubbed her cheek, still feeling the sting of that last imprint, the ragged burn of hooked nails dragging over flesh.

Corrian settled beside her, the long black ends of his coat flaring out either side, knees together, long bony fingers – nails hooked and as black as her aunt's had been – laid on his lap.

'Are you happy?' he asked again, voice soft, like feathers.

'Yes,' she said, but her voice was a whisper, hesitation and guilt thick in her throat.

Corrian cocked his head, a sharp sideways movement that looked strange on a human neck. He stared at her, eyes black as his nails, the iris swallowing the white until only a thin rim of it remained. He stared at her and didn't move, the sharp slashes of his eyebrows half raised. There was no reproach on his brow, no disbelief or anger, nothing but patience.

Tension shivered up her back, made her shoulders tight and her feet restless. She looked away, away from Corrian, away from the ruins of the house, seeking out the hypnotic spin of Old Lady Anise's windmill in the distance.

'You are not happy,' Corrian said. She felt the garden bench's old slats shift with his weight, and the absence of his stare like a laser shifted from her shoulders. 'It is okay, humans are often conflicted.'

'I'm not conflicted. She was... she was a...' She wanted to say "monster" or "devil", even just "evil" but the words caught in her throat, bottled up behind that last memory of her aunt, the way the fire had run up her legs. So fast. The blue-green flames wound around her waist, her shoulders and head, and then *whomp* it consumed her, not so much burning as collapsing in on itself before eating its own tail, sucking her aunt into the book.

Niyha's fingers itched, the urge to trace over the letters hewn into the leather strong.

She was free now, free of her aunt, free of the house and yet... and yet—

A thick brown twig nudged the book out of reach.

'Best to leave that.' Corrian nudged the book a little farther away. 'Perhaps best to let the earth have it, hide your aunt away, safe in the soil.'

Niyha nodded. The thought of knowing it was here, her aunt's evil bound in the old, crumbled pages, made her skin crawl.

'And what of the—' She was going to say "house" but a shift in the breeze brought the scent of ashes and she stopped herself. 'What of the land? What will I do with that?'

It was hers now, by both human law and witch, written down in ink and blood, plain and bold. Every worthless inch, from the old wrought-iron gate out front to the thin ribbon of the creek out back, and the book sinking into the soil.

The thought of it, of what she'd done for it...

The text on the journal writhed, and for a second Niyha sensed her aunt reaching out to her, hand wreathed in blue-green flames.

Oh Goddess. She thought confining her aunt in the journal would free her, but now... The blood rushed from her face, leaving the ice of dawning horror behind. No one would buy the land, and without money Niyha couldn't afford to leave, stuck her as surely as her aunt was in the book.

Corrian looked up, sharp, sudden, like he hadn't thought that far ahead, but she knew better. Crows always had plans within plans, they were Morrigan's favourite for more than their mastery of chess.

'We will pay you.'

'What?'

Corrian nodded, a strange double bob more suited to a bobble-head than a humanoid. 'Yes, we will pay you for the land. One hundred stones and you will fly away like you would have if she had not been.' He nodded again. 'Yes, it is settled.'

'What? But—'

He hummed, low in his throat, the sound a trill away from being a song, a serenade to welcome in the morning. Other hums rose from the surrounding trees, shadows passing over the hothouse's old, frosted glass ceiling.

Magic played over her skin – the gentle silken flutter of wings buffeting her cheeks, the prick of talons through her shirt, the musty scent of feathers in her nose – and then it was gone. Where the book had been was a pile of brilliant glittering stones, opals of every size, shape and colour, some as small as her pinkie others large as a twenty-cent piece, and one... Her fingers trembled, made the rising sun dance under the opal's skin, lighting it up like the ocean caught in the stone, shards of teal playing in the dark blue depths of its heart.

The tear-drop shaped gem fit into her palm, whispered of distant places.

'Corrian.' She breathed his name, wonder and gratitude trying to fight through the shock and fear in her voice. 'This is too much, these opals are worth a fortune.'

He shrugged, and in that moment as he shifted his shoulders and shuffled his feet, she glimpsed the crow's stark black plumage under his form. 'They are stones,' he said. 'We cannot eat them.'

He shifted again, the blue-black sheen of feathers flashing in the dawn light as he wriggled on the bench. He looked skyward, and she read impatience in the snap of his movement.

She closed her hand around the blue opal and held it to her heart. 'Thank you.'

Corrian smiled, his human form fading in a swirl of mist and wings, leaving just the trill of his voice and feather behind. 'Fly, little bird,' he said. 'Fly.'

OF CROWS
&BEASTS

INTRODUCTION

One of the great things about being a writer is the ability to rewrite the stories, movies, games and/or TV shows you thought were great until someone messed them up. It's the ultimate do-over, where you take the kernel of an idea, twist it all around and spit it back out with your own spin and your own ideas.

Of Crows & Beasts is one of those stories, although it didn't turn out quite the way I planned, not least of which is due to the conclusion, as much as it can be called a conclusion.

Alas, by the time I hit the mid-point of the story, *Of Crows & Beasts* had turned away from the original idea of a rewrite and into something else. Something bigger and meaner, much like the main character herself.

If you want to hear more, including behind-the-scenes tidbits from the writing of *Of Crows & Beasts*, check out the *Short Bits Volume 1* audio commentary.

Scan the QR code for the audio commentary.

OF CROWS & BEASTS

She got off the bus, just another tired, drawn face in another line of refugees aching from the long journey on battle-scared roads.

She tilted her head to the sky, letting the hood fall back.

At least she was free.

And if all that freedom had left her was the dark-grey clouds and damp, frigid winds of the great north's most miserable nation, she would take it.

Take it and be glad.

There were worse things than poverty, greater hardships than death. She should know, she'd run away from both.

A shove from behind; a low, grunted admonishment to 'keep moving' shook her out of her reverie and toward the tall, razor-topped fence. The thick chain-link mesh rippled with power, both electric and magical, the two forces curling around each other in a rich pattern of sparks. If she unfocused her eyes, let herself slip into the ethereal – just a shave, just enough to see under the surface of things – the riotous play of wind-drawn electricity and spell-work rolled out before her.

On the surface it was a simple warding, flashy and menacing but without any real bite. A well-enough trained Imperial mage caption would shred it in a moment, and that's where the danger lay, in the enemy's arrogance.

In *her* arrogance, that's how Laspar's forces had found her last. Why her brother was dead.

Her arrogance.

She tugged the hood back over her platinum hair and shuffled forward.

Ahead, personnel in the Spulorian army's blue and grey uniforms stood either side of rectangular identity scanners, while at their backs lurked the hulking menace of armed troops, faces hidden behind the impenetrable black shield of their helmets.

The line moved. She shuffled forward.

The endless *shuffle shhlop* of feet on the muddy ground, the quiet patter of the relentless drizzle that had pursued them over the Spulorian border, the cry of an infant and the soldiers' quiet requests for 'Documents?' and 'Step this way' were the only sounds.

None of the waiting refugees spoke, not even to murmur to the children clutched in their arms or to pass secrets to their loved ones.

That's what made the squeal of the ident scanner so loud. It split the air, a knife to her ears, burrowing right through cartilage and bone, all the way to her soul. The pain—

Oh, Goddess, the pain! It ripped through her brain, set fire to her flesh and liquified her bones.

She could not scream, could not fall, could not clamp palm to her head and cry out as so many others did, as the unfortunate in the screaming identity scanner was.

She had to stand, had to walk, had to watch as the faceless combat soldiers came alive, and Crows descended on the wildly flashing rectangle.

The black-clad operatives materialised in the air above, the long ends of the ground-sweeping coats flared about their legs as they landed, knees bent to absorb the drop, gloved hands spread. They appeared not just around the scanner – one of their number already hauling the refugee to their feet – but within the crowd, gazes already seeking, scanning.

They stalked the queues. Glossy black shields covered their heads, leaving just the long, serious slash of their lips exposed. They swung their attention left then right. Fear rolled before them, ripping through the silent masses, raising the hair on necks, and fingers in signs of warding.

The ident arch still made its flesh-sawing wail even though the one who caused it was gone – all the better to allow the Crows to find other magic-users in the crowd.

The refugees on the ground, curled into foetal balls as pain wracked their insides, disappeared in a swirl of long coats. Those that flinched or crouched or clasped hands to their ears, like they could stop their brains leaking out, were quietly moved to another, shorter line where the personnel held not clipboards or guns but glowing threads of magic.

The Crows drifted down the queue, drawing closer, one on either side of the line in which she stood.

Her bones burned, her hands ached, her teeth bit into her tongue.

The man ahead shuffled forward.

It took everything she had to lift a foot, to shove the command through screaming nerves, to not stumble, to not cry, to keep her hands clamped around the strap of her bag and not her belly.

Shuffle. Sploosh.

Shuffle. Sploosh.

The line grew shorter. The distance with it.

Shuffle. Sploosh.

The Crow on her right stalked closer, the glossy black of their faceplate sweeping over the crowd.

Five steps.

Four.

Two.

The Crow was there, attention skimming left then right. She didn't flinch, didn't cower or turn her head. For a moment, she forgot to breathe, trusting to the depth of her hood, the enveloping sexless black of her clothes, as worn and forgettable as the rest.

And then the Crow was past.

She breathed, willed relief to shed the pain from her bones, except what came out of her lips was too loud, more moan than exhalation.

A Crow in her face, long gloved fingers reaching for her hood, his helmet a mirror, reflecting her widening eyes, the long straight cut of her nose, the hollow planes of her cheeks.

Ythys, Mother of Stars, protect me now, she prayed as the hood fell to her shoulders.

The Crow said nothing, merely stared and she stared back, seeing only herself – pale amber skin turned to straw in the gloom and drizzle – and the serious, downturned corners of the Crow's mouth.

She clamped her pain and the power tight inside of her as that blank gaze bore through her soul—

A scream, inhuman. Blood curdling.

Over the other side of the yard, before the mage scanner, a demon wearing the ragged remains of human flesh roared. Talons tore into one mage solider while the others drew glowing swords and still another drew arcane symbols in the air.

The Crow vanished, gone in a gust of wind, following his fellows to the new threat.

Panic rippled through the refugees, the queues ripping sideways, away from the conflict—

It was over as quickly as it began. The alarm died with the demon, taking the endless agony with it.

The Crows went too, dematerialising but not gone. She could feel them, up there in the sky. Waiting.

The line shuffled forward.

Her legs were hell, muscles and bones soft as endorphins flooded her system, but she didn't stumble. Not now, not yet. Not when she was so close.

'Documents.' The young, stern-faced officer spoke without inflection.

She was at the scanner, just three steps, a forged identity and two combat soldiers between her and safety. Or as much safety as she was ever going to enjoy again. Tenuous, fragile as the lies it was built upon, but more than she'd known in a long, long time.

Fingers shaking, she reached inside her coat and drew out her ident card.

The officer took the battered bit of plastic and pressed it to their clipboard.

She couldn't see what appeared on the one-way screen projected over the board, but she didn't need to. The chip told the story of Belgin Féme, a thirty-two-year-old factory worker with a degree in art history and no family. From the heart of the Imperium's urbanised fringe, she had just enough magical aptitude to keep herself out of the slums, where her only asset would have been her face.

Lies. All of it, except, perhaps for her face.

The officer jerked their head toward the scanner. 'Proceed.'

The woman pretending to be Belgin Féme braced herself and stepped into the arch. The rectangular black box swallowed her.

An ident card good enough to fool the Spulorian system had taken skill and money, but this… The soul-shredding wail of before would be nothing.

She willed every fibre of her to stillness. *Ythys, guide me.*

In the physical world, it was a moment, two heartbeats to carry her through the half-metre of tech and magic, but in the ethereal, in the place where the divine spilled through the fabric of existence, it was an eternity.

Spells rippled over her being, sinking into the nooks and crannies, bloodhounds seeking the magic in her DNA even as the tech photographed and measured her physical form, stripping her down to the flesh. By the end of the scan it would know every inch of her skin, right down to the mole on her inner thigh, but it would not know her soul.

Ythys, don't let it know my soul.

If the ident alarm had been painful, the scan was torture, every inch of her aware of the spells ripping her apart, icy talons digging at her insides, pulling apart ethereal muscles, sinking long cold probes into her gut, her heart…

If she'd gone to the other scanner, declared herself a mage and let the Crows take her, it would be different. Everything would be different.

If she were lucky, she'd be dead.

She didn't want to die, and the other options… All she could do was endure. And pray.

The scanner released her.

Her face was drawn, pale. She felt the blood draining from it, sinking to her feet, skin turning clammy, the fear beads of sweat rising on her forehead. If the Crows saw her now, if the officers suspected…

She kept her gaze down, didn't look the officer in the face, eyes on their collar instead.

A buzzing from the officer's clipboard, and she imagined the results from the scanner flashing across the surface. A pause, weighty and deep. The woman pretending to be Belgin Féme held fatigue and the brilliant, vomit-inducing rush of endorphins at bay with the last, fragile strands of willpower. She prayed.

And prayed. And prayed.

The ident card thrust at her chest.

'Welcome to Spulor, Ms Féme.'

Relief made her bones sag, her hands clumsy as she fumbled the ID back inside her coat.

She'd made it.

Now, the real work began.

✦

Eighteen months later

The files landed on her desk with a *thud*, dislodging the paperwork from other stacks and threatening the stability of her plastic coffee cup.

A quick hand ensured the safety of her workspace from a black flood of caffeine, while another caught a teetering pile of delicate tech-paper before it slid to the floor.

The woman known as Belgin Féme looked up at the interloper.

A Crow looked back. Only the generous curve of his lips and the dark pits of his eyes visible behind the mask.

At least it wasn't the full-face shield. No staring at her own reflection.

'I need these processed.' He loomed at her side.

The man was good at looming.

He reached over her shoulder and leaned his weight on the new stack of files, like he was trying to increase their importance with his own weight. Drive them through her desk and into the System with the force of his will. Like he didn't trust her – a lowly, magic-less immigrant in the Crow's secretarial pool. Maybe he thought she was stupid.

Or worse, maybe he thought she was lying.

Féme looked away, ignored the warm, distinctive scent of sandalwood and bergamot that wound through her senses whenever this Crow was close. He hadn't worn it the first handful of times she'd seen him in the Pool, not even the first time he'd loomed over her shoulder or brushed by her in the hallway. Not even when he'd wandered through the neat lines of secretaries, trailing tension and surprise in his wake, and slapped the very first file on her desk.

She'd have known if he'd worn it, if anyone had the faintest trace left to recirculate through headquarters' enviros.

That scent reached down past everything that was Belgin Féme and tugged on the beast sleeping within.

She reached for the foot-high stack. 'Of course, sir. I'll get to it after—'

'No. Now.'

'I have other—'

He leaned closer, coat brushing against her shoulder, the breadth of him blocking out the light. She kept her eyes on the files, on the broad, gloved hand holding them down, even as anger and power stirred in her chest.

It was a game, a stupid, dangerous game. The bullying, the fragrance, a game designed to crack the facade of Belgin Féme.

'Now, Ms Belgin.'

'The files from yesterday—'

'Will wait. Get these done first.'

She would burn him to ashes, turn his insides out and make a garland of his intestines. She would rip the mask off his pretty little face, shred his coat and show the Crow what *real* power was. The stuff that made life and death and darkness. She would rip apart the very fabric of reality and raze this square, grey hellhole to the ground. She would—

She would nod and smile, but not too wide and not for too long, just a quick stretch of lips that didn't sink too deep into her eyes.

'Of course,' she said, but not too brightly and not too sharp either. Demure and helpful, efficient. A drone buzzing away at her desk, no different from the handful of others in the Pool. Simple. Trustworthy. Nothing to hide.

She reached for the first file.

His hand didn't move.

She gave the file a gentle tug.

'Sir,' she said and looked him in the eye. Trustworthy. 'I need the file.'

The plain black mask was expressionless, the full mouth drawn in a straight, emotionless line, but the Crow's eyes... Determination swirled in the mahogany depths, magic flickering like a lightning storm over the surface.

She did not look away, but allowed her eyes to widen, to let him peer deeper into her soul.

Trustworthy. She was Belgin Féme and she had nothing to hide.

Nothing at all.

Never.

Ever.

Trustworthy.

She was Belgin Féme.

Féme blinked, let fear whiten her cheeks and hunch her shoulders. 'Sir,' she said again, and tugged once more on the file.

The Crow turned away, anger or perhaps frustration tightening his jaw below the mask.

He pushed away from the desk. 'Get on with it,' he said and turned, the long tails of his black coat flaring behind him.

No one breathed. No one spoke.

Silence echoed in the Crow's wake.

Féme slipped the first file onto her desk before carefully repositioning the rest of the pile. The plain white rectangle of the workspace held a mountain range of tech-paper, organised around the clear valley of screen and board. Some of the mountains were small, some large, all precisely arranged; edges square with the workspace, sides crisp, corners sharp enough to slice flesh. Or so the other secretaries whispered behind her back and in the lunchroom.

They whispered other things too, gossiping like mother hens in soft, chittering voices that transcended the gender of the six men and women who occupied the small square space at the heart of the Crow's file room.

She pressed the thick, transparent sheet of plastic to the glowing rectangle of her board. A file flickered to life above.

A young woman stared back at her: dark brown eyes, hollow cheeks, the circles under her eyes telling a story of hardship. A migrant, another Imperial running to the dubious safety of Spulor's arms.

Féme's heart ached for her, while inside, the beast growled.

// *Riya Passerini.*

// *Level 3 magic user.*

// *Specialty: water manipulation.*

// *Processed at the North Gate and transported to Dunemouth for evaluation.*

// *Migrant number—*

She did not read it, hand working of its own accord, entering the information in the System, sending orders to the distribution centre for additional resources, checking Dunemouth's roster, requesting a water mage to fill the hole and test the woman when she arrived.

There were plenty of Riyas on Féme's desk, an endless stream of Imperial runaways shuffled here and there through Spulor's immigration system.

The ones like Riya were lucky, low-powered but strong enough to be useful, their specialties unobjectionable. Riya's life may no longer be fully her own, but there were worse things to live with than suspicion and hard labour.

She reached for the next file.

// *Mac Brankcovich. Plant mage. Level 4.*

// *Kerim Hayter. Healer. Level 2.*

// *Lamia Pfaff. Summoner. Archmag—*

Lamia Pfaff.

Féme froze.

Lamia Pfaff stared back at her with a tired silver gaze, bones stark against sallow skin, lips parched by thirst, cracked and bleeding. She looked older than the thirty-two years recorded on her ident.

Maybe that was just the dirt and sleep deprivation stamped on her face, or the ragged silver hair that hung in clumps around her face, where it wasn't gone altogether.

Disease had ravaged Lamia, cancer eating away at her insides, turning the strong, stoic woman Féme had once known into a skeleton. She was surprised Lamia had lasted this long, two years since their first and last meeting. Surprised the woman hadn't taken the money and then her own life. That was what Lamia had said she wanted, to end things on her own terms.

It seemed fate, or Laspar or even Spulor had had other plans. Perhaps, even Lamia herself?

Féme forced her fingers to move. This was no time to stare, not now, not with that name and that face watching her every move.

// *Lamia Pfaff. Summoner. Archmage.*

// *Processed at West Gate.*

// *High priority. Hold for debriefing.*

// *Current location.* A black box blotted out the rest.

Was the Crow there? Was this a test? Was he even now cloaked, ready to materialise if she hesitated too long, gave Lamia more attention than she deserved?

Prickles ran down Féme's spine, a tide of warning reaching into the pit of her, picking at the bindings lashing the beast.

He wouldn't do it, couldn't do it. The only person who could expose Belgin Féme was Belgin Féme, and perhaps…

Her gaze slipped back to the woman hovering over her desk. Those silver eyes, so unlike the onyx depths of her own, reached through the screen to stab her in the heart.

Lamia knew, Lamia could expose her. But only if the Crows suspected, only if they broke the bindings—

It was a trap, it had to be a trap. The Crow was right behind her, waiting to throw off his shroud of invisibility and wrap those long, spell-binding hands around her neck. She could feel him there, his breath, the warm sandalwood and sweet bergamot.

It was a trap and yet she couldn't stop her finger from scrolling down, couldn't stop herself from tapping the black box, and drinking in the words underneath.

// *Current location: Crow Headquarters. Secretarial pool.*

Hell erupted.

✦

'She is not the archmage, Anard,' the woman spoke.

The thump of hard-soled boots on concrete, frustration ringing in every sharp *clack*.

'She is.' The same frustration in the Crow's voice, the same determination. 'I can *feel* it.'

'Anard.' The woman paused, the silence filled with the Crow's *clack clack clack*. 'Anard!' she said it again, stronger, impatience filling the cold air.

The *clacking* stopped.

The woman spoke once more. 'It's been three days. If she had a breath of magic, she would have broken in two. An archmage— Are you listening to me?'

A grunt.

The woman continued. 'An archmage would have started screaming within the first hour, no matter the spells or the shielding or the mental training. An hour, Anard. An. Hour.'

A moment of silence.

'No,' the Crow – the man called Anard – said. 'It's her, I know—'

'Look at her!' Gone was the impatience, now only anger and disgust rode the woman's voice.

Through a haze of pain, Féme sensed the weight of their gazes on her slumped form. Snakes made of razors writhed under her skin, slithering through muscle and sinew in time with the music. A soft chorus, a hundred sweet voices rising and falling in perfect harmony, whispering ancient words, their meaning lost to all but the gods.

Although now… She breathed, felt the pain in her lungs, behind her eyes, cutting into her soul. The words lodged in her psyche, a part of her. Like her bones, like her tongue, seeping into her soul even as they sliced it to ribbons.

She had wanted to scream in that first hour after the Crow had materialised behind her, a dark triumphant shadow. A null collar *snicking* closed around her neck, hard gloved hands yanking her upright, almost pulling her arms from their sockets, then marching her through headquarters down to this dark, cold cell.

She hadn't fought, hadn't grabbed the stylus from her desk and driven it through the Crow's— through Anard's eye. Hadn't shown him just how truly ineffectual a Spulorian null collar was against one such as she. Hadn't done anything except let fear soak every pore of her being as she begged and pleaded and finally demanded to know what was going on.

There had been no answers, no explanations, no questions, just the cell – five concrete sides and a magi-tech forcefield – and the music.

She'd meditated at first, closing her eyes and leaving the body behind, retreating behind her mental wall. It had worked, for a little while. She'd prayed then, prayed for strength, for luck, for the pain to end.

She counted time through the brief silences when the guards came to give her water and lead her to a bathroom. She could have escaped then, could have ripped off the null collar and run away from the voices whispering in their forgotten tongue. It would have been the end of it.

The end of everything.

But she wasn't finished yet. She hadn't even started.

She had to hang on, to persevere.

Inside the cell, strapped to the chair, she huddled inside the shell of Belgin Féme, no longer praying, no longer closing her ears to the chorus.

There was wisdom in the words, a meaning that hovered on the tip of her soul, if only she could untangle it.

The voices stopped, just… gone.

'No…' Her mouth moved, breath pushed past her vocal cords, but no sound reached her ears. She'd been so close, so very, very close…

Light pierced her eyelids, ripped away the comforting dark, the last strains of the lost language floating in her memory. Then hands, on her forearms and then her knees, the hard *shrimp* of restraints removed. Another hand on her forehead, this time a thumb lifting her eyelid, a flashlight in her eye.

She twisted sideways.

'Responsive.' The woman's voice, flat and efficient. 'Vitals good. Get her into recovery.'

Lifted onto a stretcher, the rattling *thud thud thud* of wheels hitting cracks in the floor. More lights, the *whoosh* of doors, the *ding* of an elevator. Silence, save for the rustle of cloth and the shuffle of shoes. Sandalwood and bergamot filled the air, seeped under her skin, roused the beast in her soul.

Another *ding*, more doors *whooshing*. The hum of more voices, some soft, some urgent, the harsh scent of antiseptic obliterating the other.

More movement, the stretcher's wheels smooth now, no cracks or tiles to make them *thud thud thud.*

Being lifted to another bed, a blanket laid over her, footsteps receding and then… and then…

Sandalwood.

She drew the scent deep into her lungs, let it permeate every part of her. The beast roiled, claws pressing against the thin membrane that held it down, that made it quiet. That made Belgin Féme possible.

'I know you.' Anard, warm breath brushing her ear, the weight of his hands pulling the blanket tight across her shoulders. 'You can't hide forever.'

The beast stuck a talon through the membrane and, for a moment, as Belgin Féme opened her eyes, it was Lamia Pfaff who stared out.

Her stary gaze met the mahogany of Anard's, the beast baring its teeth at the power behind the Crow's.

He flinched, the rich amber of his cheeks turning pale, but he did not look away, did not recoil or scream or shout. He hardened his jaw and stared back, the thing in his soul rising to the beast's call.

Inside, in the dark places left in her psyche, the places the lights and the murmurs and the hands hadn't touched, could never touch, the unknowable song rose.

'No yaso sä awwi.' The foreign words rolled from her tongue. *I don't need forever.*

She had time to see him frown, to witness the thing behind his gaze sit upright in response, before unconsciousness took her.

MAJA KAUR
IS NOT HER NAME

THE CHESHIRE BOOK 1

INTRODUCTION

The character of Maja Kaur, as she's now known, has had many incarnations over the years but always the same story.

I first started writing Maja many years ago (in one of those other incarnations) and you might say I cut my writing teeth chronicling her early exploits. In her (and my) younger days, she was an upright, fun-loving character until her world imploded, and then she changed and things got fun. For me, at least. Not so much for Maja.

In *Crash*, Maja's hit rock bottom (just where I like them) and this is her story out.

Maja's story will continue in future instalments, whether they'll be full-length novels or not is yet to be decided.

If you want to hear more, including behind-the-scenes tidbits from the writing of *Crash*, check out the *Short Bits Volume 1* audio commentary.

Scan the QR code for the audio commentary.

CRASH

Maja's bones were cold and her mouth was full of that dry-shit metallic taste that always came after a high. It coated her tongue in a thick mucousy carpet, gumming up her tastebuds and crawling up her nose, until she was breathing out a cloud of need. Her skin was going to start crawling next, going to shrivel and dance, doing the jig until it boogied right off her body and slinked around the dirt and rock at her feet. Something, anything to get away from the desperation gripping her insides, twisting her stomach in knots, making her heart thump and jerk in her chest.

Worse than all that, though, was the buzz in her head, the dispassionate whirl of her greyware. The input at the base of her skull humming against bone was going to drive her crazy, endlessly seeking new data to feed the fine network of military-grade processors and neural connections linking her grey matter. The magic of Imperial technology royally fucked by a little black pill.

She shivered, hugged her arms tight to her chest and tried to remember if she still had her nose or if the cold had taken it along with the heat in her bones.

Did it matter? She just had to get through this, and then it was back to the shuttle crouched behind her, the hatch open, the cargo containers stacked in the hood sucking up what little light made it through the planetoid's dull, reddish atmosphere and dust. Then she could get out of the grit and howl of the wind, get away from the pervasive cold and Merc's bird-sharp eyes, and sink into the rattle of the old ship's flight system. After that... After that she could slink back to her bunk, slide her hand into the space between bulkhead and mattress, and get back to the sweet oblivion of the pills stashed there.

Her last memory of the Kid exploded in her mind's eye, his face-splitting grin gone, bloody air bubbles instead of endless damned questions spilling out of his mouth, skinny chest crushed by a cargo crate.

She gritted her teeth and breathed, hard, her breath frosting the air under her nose. She'd promised herself. The Kid was dead and she'd promised, promised that that would be the last time she piloted while she was high, the last accident she'd cause. But the skin on the back of her neck shivered and clenched and her bones ached.

Christ, she needed a fix.

She'd just finish this, do whatever the hell it was Jonko thought needed to be done on this damn arid rock instead of the *Bakr's* cargo bay, the get back to the ship and her stash and then—

'Hey, flygirl.' A hand, hard and calloused, cupped her chin.

Maja's eyes snapped open.

Merc frowned at her, hard black gaze narrowed against the wind blowing its sea of grit, crow-dark hair salted with age and the lines in his dark-gold face carved by more than just time. 'Get it together,' he said, voice as rough as the rock under her boots. 'We're on.'

The hand fell away from her chin and she followed his gaze to the two figures walking toward them out of the orange dust haze, but her attention was drawn to the shuttle behind.

The ever-present haze obscured markings, but the distinct upward curve of the tail and sweep of the wings marked it as one of the early models from the outer systems; a nuggety cargo hauler designed to run unpatrolled shipping lanes. Long range. Cruise speed, FTL two point three. Two forward guns, one rear. Slow on the turn. Handled like a brick. A quick duck and roll, get in its blind spot. Aim just forward of the engine, three degrees to starboard. The sweet spot. Hold a beat, wait for the right moment—

'There's far enough.' Merc's voice cut through her thoughts like it cut through the wind, a sledgehammer knocking her back into the now.

The two figures stopped five metres away. One old, one young, both male and far enough away they wouldn't be throwing any punches, but close enough that she and Merc'd see it if they decided to reach for the guns strapped to their sides. Not that she'd be any use if they did, with her skin starting to crawl and her hands to shake. She didn't even have a weapon of her own; Merc'd swiped her ancient pulse gun while she'd still been jacked into the flight chair, peeling her brain out of the shuttle's systems. The most she'd be able to contribute to a firefight was a sloppy dive behind the cargo ramp.

If she didn't stumble over her own feet first.

'Those the goods?' The young one, dark and rail thin, spoke. He looked like he spent a lot of time on his hair and jacked into the nets, if the contact ports flashing on the underside of his wrists were anything to go by. He pointed at the containers in their shuttle's belly.

The containers Jonko had insisted she help Merc deliver. Like a broken-down pilot could do a better job protecting the cargo than the three heavies the woman kept on payroll.

'Those are the goods,' Merc said. 'You got the credit?'

'Cargo's already been paid for,' Young and Dark said.

Merc went still. 'That's not what I was told.'

The older one, face hard and wrinkled, spoke now. 'That's because you're part of the cargo.'

What? The thought ran through Maja's mind even as she saw the young one go for the weapon at his side. She had enough time to wonder where he'd gotten his hands on something that looked like it came out of the Imperial armoury – long and sleek, the barrel forming around his hand before it even cleared the holster – but she didn't move. Her bones were too cold, her brain too slow, thoughts too tangled.

Merc tackled her to the ground and behind the ramp. He didn't tell her to stay, didn't press the big blunt grip of her old pulser back into her hand. Instead, he disappeared around the other side of the shuttle, leaving her sitting in the dirt, alone and unarmed.

Her heart pounded. Her breath came short, and adrenalin pushed back the cold and the shakes. She drew her feet up under her until she was jammed into the crevice where ramp met rock, and shuffled over enough to peek around the edge.

Young and Dark fired. Missed.

She ducked back before he improved his aim. Closed her eyes. Listened for the crunch of his footfalls on the cold, rocky dirt. There they were. One footstep. Two. Getting closer.

She swallowed, balled her hand and wondered if she would still be fast enough, strong enough, to lay him out before he shot her. A not-so-tiny voice in the back of her head said, probably not.

Gods above, she needed a fix.

There was a thump and then the distinct bark of a kinetic weapon followed by another, louder thump.

She risked another peek around the corner.

Young and Dark was face-down in the dirt, his partner the same not too far behind him. Red stained their backs, darkened the already-red ground underneath them.

Merc crouched over Young and Dark, rifled through the man's pockets. He found something, slipped it into his own pocket, and looked up. Something passed through his gaze when it met hers. Maja thought it might have been relief, but it was gone too fast. 'Can you fly that?' He gestured over his shoulder to the shuttle.

She didn't even have to look at it. 'Yeah.'

He nodded, rose. 'Good. Let's get out of here before Jonko figures out we're not dead.'

✳

Maja threw up, heaving nothing but the memory of bile, and rested her head on the wall of the cubicle that passed for the runabout's toilet.

'Finished?'

She moved her head just enough to meet Merc's hard black gaze. He was crouched next to the toilet door, elbows on knees, looking tidy if not exactly reputable in his dark shirt and trousers. She turned back to the toilet.

'You're finished.' He grabbed her arm and dragged her with him when he rose.

Stand or be dragged. Lovely. Her knees wobbled and her stomach clenched but she stood, and then toppled into Merc when he yanked her around to face the sink and the small but shiny mirror above it.

Gods she looked awful. Sunken cheeks, sallow skin, lank hair.

Before the Kid had died, she'd stopped seeing her own reflection. Not like some sort of crazed blood-sucking creature out of myth, it had still been there in the mirror or bounced back at her in a window. Perhaps it would have been better if it had disappeared altogether, at least then others would have known her for the monster she was, would have known to stay away.

Instead, she'd let herself stop noticing. It had been easier not to notice, to let her gaze slide past the brown, lank mess of her hair, the way her eyes always looked bruised, her expression slack. If she didn't notice, she didn't have to care have to feel, have to remember.

Until the Kid died.

She noticed then. Noticed it in everything shiny enough to hold a reflection. Control panels, doors, beer. No matter how much she drank, the noticing wouldn't go away, and the caring came back and then the nightmares. Not all the way, but enough for the old her, the person she'd been before Maja Kuar, to raise her voice and make her promise. No more drugs.

Now, even though her hands shock and her skin crawled, trading the sweet white oblivion of a high for the cold in her bones and the loathing in her heart was sweeter still.

Merc shoved a cloth into her face.

Maja shoved it away.

He held the cloth up in front of her. 'You going to do it?'

She eyed him, the lines in his dark skin that spoke to experience and age, the hard line of his jaw, the set of his brows. She took the cloth.

It was cold and damp and just rough enough that she could feel it sloughing away the sweat and dirt. She wiped her neck as well and then let the cloth slide out of her hands.

Merc caught it before it hit the sink. He held it back up and gestured to her coveralls. 'The rest too.'

She frowned and might have crossed her arms if she hadn't needed a grip on the sink to steady her legs.

He stepped back and threw her the cloth.

She had to use both hands to catch it. Only the toilet's small confines and a frantic shuffling of feet kept her upright. When she was steady again, Merc closed the door, shutting her in the cubicle.

She sat on the edge of the toilet and looked down at herself. The coveralls, with their zip up the front, had fit her once, now they were loose around the middle and baggy about the shoulders. They were dirty too, the dark blue material coated in a fine film of red dust and a splash of vomit. There was vomit on her boots as well, probably from that first frantic rush to the toilet.

Maja rested her head in her hands and closed her eyes. Gods, she was tired.

The door rattled.

'No sleeping,' Merc said. 'You're not out in five, I'm coming in.'

Bastard.

She frowned, sighed, and slowly reached down to pull off her boots. The coverall came next, there was a tank and shorts beneath, but they didn't hide the jut of her collarbones or her too-skinny legs. She wasn't quite a skeleton, not yet, but she could count her ribs and her arms hadn't been this gawky since she was twelve.

Maja got to work with the cloth, and by the time she was finished it was a dull red-ish brown. She left it atop the crumpled pile of coveralls and boots.

Merc was standing in front of an open storage compartment when she came out. He cast her a glance, frowned as he ran it down her body, and threw her a new set of coveralls. 'They'll be too big until you fill out some,' he said.

Until she filled out some. Right. He sound like her— Her heart jolted in her chest and she squeezed her eyes shut. No, don't think of him.

'Where're your boots?' Merc's voice snapped her head up.

She stared for a few seconds and then gestured back toward the cubicle.

'Clean 'em. We've got people to meet.'

✳

Orana's had a view, a dark swathe of vacuum framed in rock and the wide lip of the viewport. Beacons threw shadows with every slow blink, highlighting the crags and razor-sharp edges of the asteroid's surface in red, yellow and the occasional blue. It would have been hypnotic if Maja's eyes weren't dry enough to crack, her stomach raw, and if the drink in the server's hand had looked a lot more like beer and tasted a lot less like water.

It didn't help that her skin was tight and her insides jittery, or that she couldn't help her mind wandering back to the bunk and the small stash of pills she was never going to see again. Gods, she needed a fix.

The fact that Merc'd hemmed her into the booth, almost squashing her into the high-backed little corner before she'd realised what he was doing, just added insult to injury. If her legs hadn't been quite so shaky and the drink in her hand hadn't trembled quite so much, she'd have pushed back, but as it was...

As it was, she was tired and sore and knowing her old captain had tried to... Tried to what? Kill her? Sell her? For what and why? For revenge? Old Jonko had been fond of the Kid, had almost doted on him, like some crusty old spacefaring aunt with shady stories and shadier friends. When he'd died... Maja remembered how the gun had trembled, just a little, when Jonko pointed it at her head. And the old woman's eyes had been hard and hot and mean.

Maja had had anger like that, hatred like that, aimed at her before. Just once. She hadn't been Maja then and it had been worse, so, so much worse than looking down the barrel of Jonko's pulse gun.

Merc had stopped Jonko from pressing the trigger. Maybe that was why the old woman had tried to do him in as well.

Maybe.

Next to her, Merc slumped in the booth, one arm draped across the back, the other on the table, his fingers tapping against the drink near his hand while his eyes scanned the bar.

Merc stopped tapping his fingers.

Maja looked up, followed his gaze. A body modder picked their way between the empty tables, small and slim, the sharp points of curved ears rising above their head, skin not just dark but black with the faint fuzz that said fur, and a tail behind. They slid into the booth and smiled – or maybe that was a baring of pointed teeth – and settled their hands one atop the other on the table. 'Hello,' they said.

'You're late, Faus'tian,' Merc said.

The modder, Faus'tian, didn't stop smiling but their ears dipped, just a little, and something very much like annoyance ran over their features. 'Perhaps,' they said. 'But you brought a guest.' They turned their gaze, bright gold in their dark face, on Maja.

Maja stared back and tried not to think about the nausea building in the back of her throat, or how bad she wanted a fix.

'She doesn't look so good.' Faus'tian took a deep breath, nose wrinkling. 'Or smell so good. Not like your usual, Kerril.'

Kerril? Maja looked at Merc. He didn't look like a Kerril. She wondered what his 'usual' looked liked, and what sort of chats he had with Faus'tian often enough for the modder to know what that was.

Merc's frown deepened and his fingers resumed their tapping. 'I need information.'

'Yes, you usually do.' The smile dropped from Faus'tian's face. 'What is it this time?'

Merc slid a screen across the table. The faces of the two men who'd ambushed them less than thirteen hours ago hovered above the thin sheet of biogel. 'You know them?'

Faus'tian righted the screen with the tip of a claw dark as their fur. 'Mmm, perhaps.' They cocked their head to the side and flicked an ear. 'Why do you want to know?'

'They tried to kill us,' Maja spoke, her voice thick.

'Hmm.' Faus'tian's eyes flicked to Maja, going up and down like they could see the half of her hidden beneath the table. 'I do not think so.'

Maja frowned and opened her mouth to speak, but Merc got there first. 'Why?' he said.

'They are looking for bodies, living ones. You.' They pointed a claw at Merc. 'You they might kill, too much work to take alive, but her?' Faus'tian gestured to Maja and shrugged. 'Thin, sickly. Easy prey.'

'Bodies?' Merc's arm came off the back of the booth and he rested both elbows on the table. 'What for?'

Faus'tian shrugged. 'I do not know and I have not asked, nor do I care to. These men.' They tapped the screen. 'They are the type intelligent folk stay away from. Did you kill them?'

Merc leaned back. 'Maybe. Who do they work for?'

'I do not know.'

'There's a lot you don't know.'

Faus'tian shrugged again, a supple wave of bone and muscle. 'A wise male knows his limitations.'

'And the wise female?' Maja asked,

Faus'tian cocked his head, one side of his mouth lifting in a half-smile. 'I would not profess to know.' He leaned forward. 'I like you,' he said. 'Even though you smell bad.' The modder turned to Merc. 'If you want to know who employed these men, talk to Ack'tha Ox. She has a shop on the second tier, near the docks, and a finger in every less-than-legal pie in the system.'

Merc stood. 'Thanks.'

Faus'tian purred. 'Do not thank me yet. Or,' he held up one finger, 'if you insist, why not leave your fragrant companion with me? When you come back, she will smell much nicer and if you do not come back...' He shrugged and turned to Maja, both hands palm-up. 'Well, we can discuss things then, and you will still smell much nicer.'

Before Maja could do more than feel her eyes widen and her brows move toward her hairline, Merc had a large-knuckled hand wrapped around her bicep and was hauling her to her feet. 'We're good, Faus'tian.'

The modder's smile was rueful, but there was something dark in his gaze when it met Maja's. 'I tried,' was all he said.

She frowned at him. 'Why?'

The smile slipped from Faus'tian's face and his ears flattened. 'You will see.'

Merc gave her arm a tug. 'Come on,' he said. 'We've got a woman to see.'

✳

By the time they found their way to the second tier, the itch was eating Maja alive, crawling over her stomach, her back, down her throat. It was a relief when Merc propped her in a corner and she no longer had to command her knees to hold her up.

Only Merc's hand around her throat stopped her from sliding down the wall. She didn't feel the hypostick he pressed against her neck, all she heard was a soft *huuush* before the itch abated, spreading out from her neck to her fingers and toes.

The relief was almost as good as a fix.

Merc's thumb under her chin forced her gaze up until it met his. His eyes searched hers.

She blinked at him, frowned and pulled back.

He nodded, satisfaction peeking through the grim set of his jaw.

Maja frowned a little harder, raising her hand to her neck. 'What was that?'

'Something for the craving.' He stashed the stick inside his jacket.

She watched it go, her eyes glued to the small cylinder and the tiny bulge it made in the fabric. 'How did you know?'

'About the itch?' Grimness swallowed the satisfaction in his eyes. 'It's not hard.' For a moment it looked like he would say more, like he *wanted* to say more. But then his jaw turned to granite and whatever it was, he swallowed.

The second tier near the docks was dark. Too late for carousing and too early for the work shift, the concourse was deserted, the shops closed tight. Merc turned his back to the wall and crossed his arms, gaze steady on one shop in particular, a little darker and shabbier than the rest.

He looked comfortable, like he'd staked out dark little places before. Maja wondered how long he could stand there, waiting for Ack'tha Ox to open her shop, and just how hard he would squeeze to find out why their old employer had tried to kill them.

Silence stretched, and without the itch to consume her thoughts, old ones swam to the surface. 'You don't look like a Kerril.'

'It's my name.'

'Doesn't mean it fits. I like Merc better.'

'Merc?' He looked at her. 'Because I'm a mercenary? Not very original.'

Maja shrugged. 'I'm a zoner, and you're not a mercenary.'

Merc didn't jump, but she felt the jolt that went through his muscles nonetheless. 'What?'

'You heard.'

He went back to watching the shop. 'What makes you think I'm not?'

She looked at him. 'You're staking out a deserted shop trying to figure out why your last employer tried to kill you.'

'She intended worse for you.'

'She had a reason.'

Silence. They didn't need to say his name. The Kid lingered, the memory of him choking on his own blood engraved on the back of her eyelids.

'It was a rough job,' Merc said.

'I was high.'

'Yeah,' he said. 'You were.' He turned his gaze back to the darkened shop. Silence stretched again.

A round little redhead slinked down the concourse and into the shadows that surrounded the shop.

'Looks like our woman. Stay here.' Merc strode across the concourse.

Still hidden in the shadows of their little corner, Maja watched him disappear inside the shop.

Movement caught her eye. She turned. A man in a grey-green uniform, an official-looking patch on his sleeve and a pulse gun at his side, ambled down the concourse. A security officer. His gaze met hers.

Her breath stalled. She turned away, wishing she could blend back into the shadows, instead trying to make her shoulders relax and herself look inconspicuous, but her shoulders felt like steelcrete and there was a fine tremor in her hands. Out the corner of her eye, she saw the officer pause and braced herself when he started toward her.

She'd done nothing wrong, there was no reason for the officer to arrest her, but Maja's eyes still scanned the concourse, looking for an escape route.

That was when Maja saw her.

Jonko.

The old woman strode down the concourse, her lined, dusky face pressed into a scowl, her hard-soled boots click-clicking on the floor, salt-and-pepper hair tied back, the end bouncing with each step. With a bear-shouldered heavy at her back and the unmistakable bulge of a gun under her coat, Maja had no doubt Jonko had come expecting trouble.

And she was headed straight for the shop.

Maja looked behind her. The officer was looking at her, a frown starting to crinkle his brow. He was still a few strides away, she could get away before Jonko saw her, take the shuttle and be anywhere but there in a day, an hour, a minute. She leant her head against the wall and gritted her teeth, thought of Merc, of the way he'd dispatched the two goons back on Turak. He could take care of himself and gods above, she thought, her last memory of the Kid flashing through her mind, she'd done worse than leave a man she barely knew in the lurch.

It was a pity the thought didn't stop the roil of her stomach.

Maja's hands clenched, her breath came short, and with a last look at the security officer, she pushed off the wall and strode toward the shop.

One stride, two, three. She thought she heard something – an indrawn breath, a curse, the clatter of Jonko's hard-soled boots coming to a dead stop – whatever it was, Maja looked up, her eyes catching Jonko's. The old woman's eyes, a startling emerald green in her dusky face, widened a split second before her mouth clenched and she reached for the gun.

Maja ran. Heard Jonko shout. Eight long strides and she was across the concourse – heart pounding, breath rasping in then out – her palm slamming into the doorplate. There was time enough to glance over her shoulder, to see Jonko and the heavy pounding toward her, to hear the security officer yell, before the door whooshed open.

She was inside, fumbling for the lock before her eyes had time to adjust to the dark. When they did, and the door had locked behind her, her breath stopped in her throat.

The shop was a mess. Wares littered the floor, boxes and bottles and things that her eyes couldn't identify, some smashed, most not. And standing in the middle of it all, blood tricking from a split lip, his hands fisted at his sides, was Merc, his gaze fixed on the redhead pointing a gun at his chest.

'Captain Jonko, right on time,' the woman, Ack'tha, said, without taking her eyes from Merc.

Merc's eyes flicked to Maja's. Grim determination had narrowed his gaze, but when it met hers, an ugly smile stretched his lips.

'That's not Jonko,' he said.

For a heartbeat, Ack'tha was still. Then she moved, head swivelling first, gun following.

For Maja, there was time enough to see the beginnings of a bruise over Ack'tha's eye, to identify the gun – an MTF7-80, standard ImpMit issue – to see Merc move, too slow and too late to tackle Ack'tha in time.

✳

Ack'tha's gun loomed large.

Maja's heart stopped, her eyes went wide, and for one split second there was nothing in the galaxy but that gun, slowly moving to point at her heart.

Something clicked in her brain then. She moved, the motions flowing through her muscles without thought. Step out, slide in. Grip. Twist. Ack'tha's fingers spasmed, the gun falling from her grip. Maja was still moving, rolling her back into the woman's body, lifting her elbow up, slamming it into Ack'tha's face. There was a crack and a cry, but Maja kept moving. Stoop, spin.

The hard contours of the gun's handle felt familiar in Maja's hand. She rose, the weapon trained on Ack'tha even as the woman stumbled backward, hands cupped over a broken nose.

Merc appeared at her side, his split lip and swelling eye mute testament either to a lucky shot on Ack'tha's part or the woman's brawling skills. From the shattered bottles and scattered bric-a-brac cluttering the tiny shop's floor, Maja suspected the latter.

Even backed up against a bench, her hands over her nose and a gun pointed at her face, Ack'tha still held Maja's gaze with a steely one of her own. 'Nice move, girly. Seems to me you're not as washed up as Jonko thought.'

Merc grabbed Maja's shoulder. 'You were going to stay outside,' he said.

She was, until she'd seen their old employer walking down the concourse. 'Jonko's here.' Maja's voice shook and she hated it. She breathed deep.

Merc paused. Looked at her. 'You're sure?'

She adjusted her grip on the phaser and nodded.

Merc swore.

She thought of the bear-shouldered heavy that'd been at Jonko's back, and distaste coated the back of her tongue. 'She's got Smithon with her,' she added, the shake not so bad now.

Merc swore harder, then his jaw turned to stone and he stalked toward Ack'tha, blood now dripping from between the fingers still cupped over her nose. 'The goods Jonko was delivering in the Turak system. Who was the buyer?'

'You mean, who was she selling *you* to?' Even through the blood trailing over her upper lip, Ack'tha smiled, and for a moment Maja thought the woman wasn't going to answer. 'Nuary Iral. Not that that will do you much good,' she said, still smiling.

'Why?' Maja said.

"Cause it's not his real name, sugar plum.' Ack'tha tilted her head back and took her hand away from her nose. 'And because your old captain's going to be breaking down that door any second now. She was right pissed you know, when she asked me to broker that deal, and not over the terms. What'd you do? Scratch her ship?'

Merc moved, hand clamping around Ack'tha's throat, pushing her face into the bench. 'Does it matter?'

Ack'tha croaked and managed an awkward shrug. 'Suppose not,' she said, her voice strangled.

A thump made Maja's stomach jump. Another thump and the muffled sound of someone demanding they open the door added a spike of fear to the mess in her belly.

Merc shoved his face in close to Ack'tha's. 'Tell me how to contact Nuary Iral.'

Ack'tha laughed. 'Hang around another minute. I'm sure me and Jonko can arrange for you to have a real up-close-and-personal.'

The door screeched, making Maja's heart kick. She glanced back at it, and her heart kicked again at the thin line of air between it and the frame. Jonko was already forcing her way in.

'Merc,' Maja said, a quiver in her voice. A quiver. She hated the quiver more than the shakiness, hated the queasy mire of fear out of which it rose. That wasn't her, or maybe it was, maybe it had been her all along and that was why—

Maja took a breath, in through the nose, out through the mouth – *steady*, she told herself, *steady* – and swung the gun from Ack'tha toward the gap in the door. Gods, she needed a fix.

Merc growled, and a shard of darkness appeared in his grip and pressed into the pale gold of Ack'tha's throat. More of the woman's blood beaded against the matt-black blade. 'I don't have time for games.'

Ack'tha coughed, the whites of her eyes showing but her teeth still clenched in a snarl. 'No, you don't, so get going before you and your stung-out slag end up in body bags.'

'Don't worry.' Merc jerked the woman to her feet, taking his knife away from her throat only long enough to swing her in front of him so they were both facing the door. 'I'll make sure Jonko hits you first. Give me the contact.'

'Ain't nothing to give.'

The door screeched again, the gap widening. Maja's hand flexed around the weapon's grip. Then, through the gap, Maja caught a glimpse of the patch on a security officer's uniform.

Ack'tha laughed, her eyes on Maja. 'You going to shoot up colony security, sugar plum?'

Maja's stomach roiled, uncertainty joining the mess of fear. She took a breath. 'Merc.' The quiver was still in her voice. She took another breath. 'We need to go.'

'Yeah? Where?' Merc's face was grim. 'There's no back door.'

No back... Maja took a closer look around the shop, beyond the mess left by Merc and Ack'tha's brawl. It was barely even a shop, just a poorly lit room without so much as a window let alone a back door. Her gaze locked with Ack'tha's and the hate and glee in the woman's eyes confirmed Merc's words.

There was only one thing to do.

She was at the door in two easy strides, her back plastered to the wall beside the gap, her thumb gliding over the ImpMit-issue gun's controls. The soft vibration as she switched it to stun was as familiar to her as the way her lungs expanded on the single deep breath she took before she hit the door lock.

The security officer was down before the door finished whooshing open. Smithon went next, the heavy's gun barely level with her chest before he crumpled. Out the corner of her eye she saw Jonko, closer to the door.

Maja popped out of the doorway, aiming for centre mass. The shot went wide. Jonko fired back, even as she slid into a recessed doorway farther up the concourse.

There was movement beyond Jonko as more security officers ran down the concourse toward them.

A thump from behind drew her attention back into the shop. Ack'tha lay on the floor at Merc's feet, eyes closed, blood crusting around her nose. She didn't look dead but—

She didn't see Merc at her side until he jerked her sideways. The flash and the scorch mark where her head had been was all she needed to know about Jonko's aim.

Merc snatched the gun from her hand, firing as he popped his head out the door. Gold bursts joined the red ones from Jonko's weapon. The security officers were getting closer.

'We have to make a run for it,' Maja said.

Merc's face was beyond grim, his mouth a single flat line, his jaw tight, his eyes dark. For a second, he didn't say anything, just looked at her while more streaks of red and gold scorched the doorframe.

He nodded, grabbed her arm and then they were out the door, dashing across the concourse while gun shots burned around them.

✳

Colony security was waiting for them at the shuttle.

After three hours of slipping through forgotten corridors,

avoiding patrols and surveillance cams, Maja's skin was crawling and her brain has been consumed by the itch. Which was why she ran into Merc's arm, thrust outwards, before she stumbled onto the main concourse. Her breath left her lungs with a sharp 'oof'.

That one arm pinned her against the wall of the service corridor while Merc craned his neck around the corner. When he turned back, his face was harder than usual although not as hard as when he'd had that knife against Ack'tha's throat.

Maja was glad of the arm, or as glad as she could be with the itch shrivelling her skin, her insides aching and that metallic dry-shit taste entrenched in her tastebuds. Whatever little miracle Merc had given her earlier was long gone, and the need had slammed right back in its place.

Gods, she needed a fix. A small one would do it, just a taste to warm her bones and steady her hands. Just one.

She leant her head against the wall. Flicked her eyes to Merc – tendons in his neck strained as he peered around the corner – then to the tiny bump over his chest where he'd stashed his little miracle.

Maja licked her lips. That was what she needed. Just a taste...

Merc swore, hand hard on her forearm as he trotted back the way they'd come. 'Come on.'

She stumbled, her feet heavy. He caught her before she face-planted, and her hand found the small bump in his chest pocket. She licked her lips again, fingers curling over the vial like she could dig through the material. Maja breathed deep. 'I need that,' she said.

Merc gripped her biceps, hauled her upright and tried to keep walking. 'No, you don't.'

Maja didn't move. 'Yeah, I do.'

Merc was in her face, hauling her heels off the floor before she could blink. 'No.' His face was a snarl, and he shook her with each word. 'You. Don't.'

They were the same height, but with her heels off the floor she was looking down at him, just a little, and his eyes were hard and hot and so very, very angry. Her heart stuttered and her breath stopped. For a second, Merc's face morphed into another – older, leaner, with the same brown eyes as hers – and panic bloomed in her chest.

She swung at him, or tried to. With Merc holding her upper arms tight against her ribs, all she managed was a weak uppercut, but her knee found better purchase.

Merc dropped her.

Panic still making her heart pound, Maja stumbled backward, eyes on Merc, now doubled over and cupping his groin. Her feet caught up on themselves and she fell, landing on her arse in the junction where the service corridor met the main concourse.

For several long moments, all she heard was the blood in her ears and all she saw was that other face, the one in her nightmares, laid over Merc's. Maybe that was why she missed the first shout.

Movement, caught in the corner of her gaze, made her turn. An officer in a green-grey uniform with a security patch on their shoulder, ran toward her, and behind them... Maja scrambled to get her feet under her. Behind the officer came Smithon – Jonko's bear-shouldered heavy – and the snarl on his face was enough to make Maja's gut shrivel.

Maja was on her feet, heart pounding louder than before. She tore her gaze from Smithon, found Merc's. His eyes weren't angry anymore, although his mouth was a single hard line and his brows made another, darker one on his forehead. Instead, there was something else in them, something that looked like fear.

He was a step toward her, his hand outstretched.

She took a step toward him; didn't feel the shot that felled her.

※

A million dagger-footed ants crawled over her skin, and Maja groaned as she woke, rolling onto her side and curling around the nest that bloomed over her ribs. Whoever shot her hadn't been kind. Or maybe it was just the itch. Maybe it was both, the aftereffects of the stun ricocheting off the need for another hit until her fingertips stung and her toes buzzed and all the parts in between screamed and writhed and crawled.

She groaned again, reaching for the edge of the hard cot as her stomach heaved.

Someone, somewhere, clapped.

Spitting out the last bit of bile, her eyes watering, Maja looked up.

She recognised the broad glowing lip of a cell before she caught the tell-tale shimmer of the force field. If her skin hadn't been crawling, she probably could have recognised where she was from the smell alone. No matter how they sanitised them or how they didn't, jails always smelled the same, like sweat and stale air and, in her case, vomit.

Smithon grinned at her from the other side of the force field, a tall, broad-shouldered shadow, the right side of his face pulled tight by an old scar. 'Nice going, Kuar. Didn't think you had any more of that left in you.'

Maja's stomach twisted but not with the urge to heave, and her heart beat a little faster in her throat. Arms shaking, she pushed herself into a sitting position, eyes never leaving Smithon's. 'What are you doing here?'

Smithon's grin widened, the old scar pulling the right side of his mouth askew and filling his baby blues with inhuman glee. He did something on his side of the force field and the barrier vanished with a purple-white zap.

Maja's stomach twisted a little harder.

'What I always do, Kuar,' Smithon said.

A bucket clattered across the floor, skidding in the vomit.

He followed the bucket in and leaned against the wall. 'I'm making sure you don't choke on your own spew, at least until Jonko gets her hands on you. You can clean up that though.' He jerked his chin toward the mess on the floor. 'I got standards.'

Maja didn't move, save to wipe the last bit of spit and bile from her face with the arm of her coveralls. Her heart pounded, but she breathed – once, twice – and her voice stayed steady. 'Where's Jonko?'

'She's coming. Frankly, I thought you'd be more concerned about old Kerril.' Smithon shoved off the wall and took the three strides to the cell's hard cot. He sat, so close his thigh brushed hers.

Maja tensed, dragging herself as far away from him as possible. If she could have trusted her legs, she'd have stood and made a move for the still de-activated force field. But her feet were full of pins and needles and she doubted she'd do more than fall on her face, and that would just give Smithon an excuse to touch her.

She eyed Smithon's hands, curled loosely on his knees with palms big enough to cover her face and short, pudgy fingers she'd seen carve into a still-squealing vole with the dexterity of an artist.

Smithon whistled. 'That old merc can move.' He leaned in against her side until his breath filled her face. 'He wasn't going to leave you behind you know, at least not until I shot him. Not full on, just a glancer, right here.' He jabbed Maja's shoulder with a finger she felt all the way to the bone. 'Probably should've had my girl set to kill, but I made him drop his weapon, probably made his whole arm numb for a good hour too.

'Besides.' Smithon bumped her shoulder with his beefy one. She tried to lean away, but he had her wedged against the wall. 'The captain wants you alive.'

Carefully, her eyes as much on the open cell as they were on Smithon's hands, she uncurled her legs from the cot. 'Killing me'd be easier,' she said. She struggled to keep her voice steady but it wobbled all the same.

'But not as profitable, and between you and me, the captain's got a few debts. Besides,' Smithon pushed his face in close to hers, 'she wants to see you squeal.' He grinned.

Maja's heart stopped.

He laughed and slapped her leg, his hand wrapping around her thigh like a vise. 'But don't you worry, I'll be there to make sure you don't choke.' His hand squeezed. 'At least for the first little bit.'

Fear spiked in her belly, traveling all the way up her spine and jamming itself into her brain. She would have liked to say that it was skill and cunning that did the rest, but it wasn't. Panic triggered the response and adrenalin drove her muscles. It was only long-forgotten training that guided her hand, pulling back her fingers before her palm slammed into Smithon's nose.

There was a crack. A bright spurt of blood.

Maja was off the cot, stumbling over the bucket and slipping in the vomit before Smithon howled. She felt more than saw his hand reach for her. The bucket handle was in her grip as she stumbled back to her feet, Smithon's fingers brushing against her back. She planted her feet. Swung.

The bucket made a hollow thud when it hit Smithon's face. He fell, collapsing sideways on the cot, and didn't move.

Maja paused a second, breathing hard, eyes wide and heart beating madly. He was still breathing, his chest rose and fell, but that was all. She dropped the bucket and had her hands up under Smithon's coat before it hit the ground.

Smithon had once boasted that he never went anywhere unarmed, not even the shower. She hoped it was true as she ran her hands over his chest and behind his back. A gun, a knife, a freaking wrench, she'd take anything if she could just find it.

She had to get out of here before Jonko came back, before Smithon came to.

The small pistol was tucked into his boot. Maja fumbled it out, the pins and needles in her hands almost gone but lingering just long enough to make her fingers feel like wood.

There was only one other cell in the small jail, and it was empty and the doorway that connected it to the security office open. Unease disrupted the acidic boil of fear and panic long enough to stop her rushing headlong through the door. This wasn't right. Her gut screamed it at her.

Maja breathed deep and forced herself to think. Smithon being careless enough not to reactivate the force field she could believe, but this...? Her spine crawled and she swung around, the tiny pistol clutched in both hands, but Smithon still lay on the cot, only his chest moving.

She turned back to the open door and slowly, weapon held before her, moved forward. By the time she peeked around the doorframe, her heart was pounding. The security office was empty. There was a console in front of her. She'd have to go around it to get to the door on the other side.

Maja crept forward, back still crawling and her palms beginning to sweat. Unease had a firm grip on her spine, rippling up and down her vertebrae, making her breath come fast and her head dizzy.

She was around the console, her eyes locked on the door. She could see movement beyond it, a crowd of some kind. Just another metre, that's all she needed.

A weight slammed into the middle of her back.

✳

Maja fell, pistol skittering from her grasp, chin hitting the floor hard enough she saw stars.

Hands, big hard hands strong enough it felt like they would crush her ribs, flipped her over.

Smithon snarled down at her.

She swung at him.

He punched her in the face.

More stars. For a moment, a minute, or maybe it was an hour, there was nothing. Her head was hollow, her ears numb and it seemed she had an eternity to marvel at the pricks of light clouding her vision. Then there was the smell of blood, and pain shooting from her nose, lining her eye-socket in fire and her cheekbone in more of the same.

Smithon blocked out her vision, lips pulled back over his teeth, blood still running from his own nose and the gash in his hairline, the old scar on his face puckered and mean. He slammed her into the floor. 'It wasn't nice, Kuar, hitting me with that bucket, or in the nose.' He slammed her into the floor again. 'You're meant to be nice.'

There were spots in her vision, great splotches spreading across her eyes, saturating the world with light and colour. She breathed, choked on blood and tried again. 'Says who?' she spat out.

He shoved his face right in Maja's, and the blood dripping down his face dripped onto hers. 'Says me.'

Maja didn't just bite Smithon's nose, she wrapped her teeth around the already broken flesh and tore.

Smithon howled. Reared back,

A chunk came off in her mouth. There was barely enough time to spit it out before Smithon's hands were around her neck, squeezing.

She clawed at his hands, at his face, fingertips slipping in blood, feet thrashing at the floor as her lungs began to burn.

Smithon squeezed tighter.

Maja's vision blackened, her lungs going from burning to screaming.

Smithon grinned.

A bright burst of light.

Smithon's face went slack, his fingers loosened. He toppled sideways.

Maja breathed, air filling her lungs in a ragged gasp.

Her eyes lighted on Jonko, standing where Smithon had been.

The old woman glared.

Maja flipped over onto her belly and scrambled for the stolen pistol.

A red bolt hit the floor a micron from Maja's fingertips. 'Get up.' Jonko's voice was hard and flat.

Maja didn't move.

'Now.'

Slowly, Maja got up. Her head swam when she straightened and a fresh flow of blood trickled from her nose.

'Turn around.'

Just as slowly as she had stood, Maja turned, a whisper of fear curling around her spine.

Jonko's gaze was as hard as her voice, her steel-grey brows drawn tight, her mouth a single flat line. The gun in her hand didn't waver.

'I should have killed you after that last run.'

The last run, the one that killed the Kid. Once again, her last memory of him flashed before her, lying on his back, blue eyes wide, his chest flattened by a cargo container.

Maja's voice was thick, her nose blocked by blood and broken bone. 'Why didn't you?'

The old woman's mouth twisted. 'Wish I knew. Conscience perhaps, or Kerril's smooth bloody tongue? Take your pick.' She looked over Maja's shoulder. 'Restrain her,' she said.

Maja jumped when hands yanked her wrists behind her body. She tried to turn, but all she caught was a glimpse of a grey-green uniform and black hair before the handcuffs clicked into place and she was shoved forward.

'After our little firefight this morning, it wasn't difficult to persuade colony security to lend me a few hands.' The muzzle of Jonko's gun pressed into Maja's collarbone. The old woman stepped in close and the look in her eyes chased a shiver down Maja's spine. 'This particular officer is going to escort us to the docks. While we're walking there, I want you to try something, anything to escape, because then I'm going to stun you, drag you back here and let Smithon finish choking the life out of you.'

Maja leaned back as Jonko leaned closer, leaned farther back until she was pressed up against the officer behind. There was something in the captain's eyes, a rabid gleam that chilled Maja's blood more than her words.

She swallowed. 'I thought you'd made a deal with Nuary Iral.'

Jonko snarled. 'Screw Iral. I regretted that deal as soon as I made it. Watching you die is worth ten times the amount he's wiping off my debt.'

'So why not break it?' Even as she spoke the words, a little voice in the back of Maja's head said, don't.

'Because I'm a woman of my word. Something you,' Jonko pressed the disruptor harder against Maja's chest, 'wouldn't know squat about. But if you make trouble...' Jonko laughed, an ugly sound that twisted Maja's stomach. 'Well, then that's just fine.'

'Captain Jonko.' The security officer behind Maja spoke. 'If we do not go now, we will be late to meet Mr Iral. He does not like to wait.'

The officer's voice was familiar, and Maja frowned and tried to twist around for a better look, but a hand on the back of her neck kept her facing forward.

Jonko sneered at the officer and then at Maja. 'The perky little hairball's right. Iral never did have any patience, always wanted what he wanted then and there. It always made me wonder how he made it to the top of the heap.' She looked over Maja's shoulder and jerked her head toward the door, speaking to the officer. 'You know the way. Since Smithon's down, looks like I'm taking the rear.'

'Of course.' With his hand still on the back of Maja's neck, the officer spun her around and shoved her toward the door.

Maja was pushed through the main security office where the eyes of the people within widened at the sight of the blood crusting around her nose, before their gaze fell on the officer behind her and they looked away. It was the same on the winding hallways, the lift that emptied as soon as it opened, and the crowd of passengers who saw them. The concourse that lead to the docking ring was worse, with more people to stare and point and whisper. Some even jeered as Maja was marched past.

Through the mess of adrenalin and the cold chill of fear, humiliation churned in her stomach. She jerked at the security officer's grip.

He tightened his grip on her neck, and the sharp tips of what could only be claws made her stumble to a halt. He grunted and pushed her forward again. 'Do not tempt the captain to shoot, *karrumbra*, it would be most inconvenient.'

The voice, the claws, the hair. Even as she let him push her forward, an image formed in Maja's mind, of a small black modder weaving his way through a bar. Faus'tian?

✳

Where was Merc? Faus'tian was at Maja's back, playing at being a security officer as he marched her toward the docking ring, while Jonko followed two steps behind.

Where were they going, and what was waiting for them there? An ambush? Why hadn't the modder shot Jonko already? They could escape into the crowded concourse.

They turned, and the crowd was gone. Instead, they faced a docking bay, a small beige semi-circle carved out of the main thoroughfare, with two large viewports bracketing an airlock. Outside the airlock, Maja made out the flat triangular hull and stubby thrusters of an old ImpMit scout, while inside a man waited for them.

Tall enough to stare Maja in the eye, with the round cheeks and soft belly of someone who spent his off time eating, the man sent a shiver down Maja's spine. Nuary Iral's gaze wasn't cold, it was dead and buried and his eyes, running down her body made her wish she was on the other side of the airlock.

Maja tried to step back but Faus'tian, small though he may have been, was a solid wall behind her, his grip tightening on her neck, the tips of his claws pricking the skin. She wasn't going anywhere.

If he noticed her discomfort, Iral gave no indication. Instead, he looked right through her to the dark-haired woman bringing up the rear. 'Captain Jonko, I paid you for two.'

Maja didn't have to see her ex-captain's face to picture the scowl twisting the old woman's brow. 'Can we discuss this inside, Iral? The docks have ears.'

The man didn't so much as frown. 'The ears know better than to listen. Where's the other one?'

Silence. Maja pictured the lines on Jonko's forehead deepening with her scowl. 'There were problems—'

'I paid for two.' Iral turned on his heel. 'Come back when you have the other one.'

Faus'tian's grip tightened on her neck, his body vibrating against hers. She didn't need to hear him say it. This wasn't how the plan was meant to go. But why, what better chance than this did he and Merc have of pulling her arse out of the fire? Unless—

She didn't get a chance to finish the thought.

There was a growl, a human one, and then the shhh-zap of a disruptor.

A weight against Maja's back pushed her forward. Even as she stumbled, her heart stopped. Faus'tian's grip on her neck loosened, and the modder slid down her body. When she turned, he was a small black lump at her feet.

Not working for Jonko then.

Jonko tucked her weapon back into her belt. 'There,' the old woman said. 'Now you have two. Can we get this done?'

'Hmm.' Iral's belly spilled over the top of his trousers when he knelt at the modder's side. He turned Faus'tian over, his hands – strong, long-fingered, with the hardened calluses of a fighter covering the first two knuckles – turning the modder's chin from side to side. 'He will do,' Iral said as he rose.

'Do for what?' The words popped out of Maja's mouth. She shuddered, and fought the urge to take another step back when Iral turned his gaze on her.

The man blinked and then he smiled, the expression barely grazing his eyes. 'You will see, Ms Kuar.' He gestured to Faus'tian. 'Carry him aboard.'

Maybe, if she could just get her hands free... Maja pulled at the cuffs restraining her hands, her heart beating hard. 'I can't.'

Without changing his expression, Iral kneeled back at Faus'tian's side and riffled through the modder's pockets. When he rose again, he held a key and twirled his finger for Maja to turn around.

She did, her heart thudding in her throat. She took a breath – in through the nose, out through the mouth – and fought to keep her hands from curling into fists. She'd have to be quick. As soon as the cuffs loosened, she'd move.

'Iral.' Jonko growled the man's name, the captain's weapon back in her hands. 'Don't be an idiot, half the blood she's wearing isn't hers.'

'Only half?' Iral's voice was expressionless.

There was a tug on Maja's wrists as Iral inserted the key. The muscles along her spine tightened. A click. Her heart skipped a beat. A beep. The cuffs loosened. Maja started to spin—

Iral's foot drove into the side of her knee.

Maja felt something tear, and then pain exploded through the joint. She collapsed, taking the impact on her forearms and barely saving herself from diving nose-first into the floor. Her breath left her in a rush, emptying her lungs of air for even so much as a moan, and for a moment pain left her blind. Her lungs expanded, the air whistling back in, but before she could force it past her vocal cords, a hard brown boot found her ribs and flipped her over.

Iral stared down at her, his round-cheeked face as hard and dead as his eyes, the cuffs held loosely in one hand. Slowly, calmly, he lifted one large boot-clad foot and ground it into Maja's injured knee.

She gasped, her vision turning white.

The pressure let up, and when she could see again, Iral was still staring down at her. 'Do we have an understanding, Ms Kuar, or shall I pop the other ligament?'

Maja blinked, gaping like a fish, and nodded.

'Good.' He nodded toward Faus'tian, still out cold. 'Carry the modder.'

Carry Faus'tian? Maja blanched. Standing was going to be painful enough. 'My knee...' she said.

'You have two.' Iral dismissed her and turned to Jonko. 'You can go.'

Gun held loosely by her side, the old woman smiled, black eyes crinkling at the corners, her teeth flashing white against dark lips. 'Oh no, I want to see this.'

Maja bared her teeth at the woman, but Jonko only chuckled.

She crawled to Faus'tian, her knee throbbing in time with her heartbeat, and gathered the modder in her arms. Taking a deep breath, her eyes closed and teeth gritted, she pushed herself to her feet. Pain turned her vision red and brought bile to the back of her throat, but she stood.

With Jonko still grinning, Maja followed Iral through the airlock and into the dark-red confines of the starship. She shambled along in his wake. Faus'tian was boneless in her arms, his weight dragging at her shoulders and adding its own special agony to that already shredding her knee.

Maja barely made it through the docking tube before she collapsed. She slid down the first bulkhead she could put her back to, Faus'tian still in her arms and sweat beading her brow.

Fighting the desperate urge to throw up, Maja barely heard Jonko's angry 'You!', or caught the bright flash of a gun before the captain's body landed at her feet.

✳

Jonko's gaze caught Maja, the old woman's eyes wide and dark. Fathomless. The burgundy interior and dim lighting of the ship's small lounge cast the captain's skin in a sickly shade of red.

She wasn't breathing.

'I trust you are duly satisfied with my end of our bargain, Mr Kerril.' Nuary Iral spoke from somewhere above her.

'Well enough.' Merc's voice, deep and gravely, jerked Maja's gaze upwards. He caught it, frowned at her and then at Faus'tian lying unconscious across her lap. 'Although I would have preferred my partner to remain conscious.'

'And I would have preferred Captain Jonko alive. It is hard to reclaim debts from the dead.' Iral bent, grabbing one of Jonko's ankles. 'If you will wait while I remove the captain and retrieve the item, we can conclude our business.'

Merc nodded.

'Excellent.' Iral strode out of the ship's small lounge, Jonko's corpse dragged in his wake.

Maja watched, her breath coming fast, until the last strand of Jonko's salt and pepper hair disappeared down the corridor. 'Why'd you kill her?'

Merc knelt, his face grim and his shoulders tight until his fingers found the pulse in Faus'tian's neck. 'She'd have kept coming after us. It was for the best.'

'I—' She didn't know what to say to that, her mind was blank, a vacuum where the memory of Jonko's dead gaze sat side-by-side with the Kid's blood-stained lips. Only the Kid's death was her doing, but they both sat in her chest, hard lumps that burned at her insides.

Maja shook her head, chasing the images into the dark corners of her mind where they would be food for nightmares. There were other things to worry about, like the bargain between Merc and the man she'd thought they were running from. 'What's going on?'

Merc's eyes snapped to hers, and she could see the tension claim him, before he gripped her chin in one large-knuckled hand. His gaze catalogued her broken nose, the livid bruises around her throat, and her right knee, swollen and useless. 'How much of this blood is yours?'

Maja jerked her chin out of his grip. 'Enough,' she said. 'Why are you with Iral? I thought he wanted us for body parts.'

'He wants other things more.'

'Like what?'

Merc was silent, his hands turning to fists on his knees. 'A field test.'

Something cold slithered through Maja's gut. 'What's he testing?'

Merc just looked at her, his brows drawn tight, his mouth hard. His gaze slid from hers and he shook his head. 'You were right, earlier today, when you said I wasn't a mercenary.' His eyes, dark and sad, found Maja's. 'The organisation Iral works for is developing a drug, something the government will never approve. It's why Iral's buying people; to use them as test subjects.'

Maja felt the blood drain from her face.

'I made a deal with Iral.' Merc grabbed her chin again, and this time Maja didn't pull away. 'He's going to let you go, but before he does... He has investors and they want a demonstration using someone outside of the lab.' He released her chin. 'I'm sorry.'

I'm sorry. The words turned Maja's insides to ice, and if Faus'tian's prone form hadn't been holding her down, she would have scrambled to her feet. Instead, she sat with her back against the bulkhead and tried to breathe around the pounding of her heart. 'Why...' she began. 'Why are you sorry?' But she knew. She knew.

He got to his feet, turning away as the door whooshed open and Iral returned, a hypostick in his hand.

Maja looked at it, looked at Merc, heart beating harder.

'Your end of the bargain, if you please.' Iral held the stick out.

Merc stared at it, jaw tightening until Maja thought it might shatter.

A frown passed across Iral's brow. 'Sooner rather than latter would be preferable, Mr Kerril.'

Merc took the stick from Iral's hand. Carefully, he bent and lifted Faus'tian from Maja's lap, propping the modder in his own corner of the cabin before returning to Maja's side.

Without Faus'tian's weight holding her down, she shifted her good leg under her and tried to stand. 'Merc, what's—'

His hand on her shoulder slowly but surely forced her arse back to the floor. 'Sorry, flygirl. This was the best I could do.'

Knots twisted Maja's stomach, and her eyes were wide on the hypostick Merc lifted toward her neck. She grabbed his wrist in one hand, but the stick kept coming. 'What's in that?'

His lips pressed tight.

'Merc?'

The 'spray touched her neck and there was a cool burst of air against her skin.

Merc sat back on his heels, his eyes tight on hers.

Maja stared back, heart pounding as she waited for... for what? She didn't feel any different. Her knee still throbbed, her throat burned and her nose was a dull ache three times too big for her face. Had Merc swapped the hypostick?

A shadow loomed over Merc's shoulder, and Maja lifted her gaze to meet Iral's. His face was impassive, but there was a gleam in his eye, a spark of curiosity mixed with anticipation. 'The nanites will take a few moments to adjust to her system, once they have, the hallucinations will begin.'

Her heart slammed hard against her chest. 'Nanites?' She looked at Merc. 'Hallucinations? What did you give me?'

'You'll be okay,' he said.

'Unlikely.' Above them both, Iral's mouth contorted into a thin smile. 'Even if you survive the injection, the effects of the drug are long-lasting and... unpredictable.'

Iral's lips twisted, and twisted some more until his mouth was a pale swirl in the midst of a face slowly turning orange. Maja blinked as she slid sideways. That wasn't right. His face should be purple.

Her shoulder hit the deck with a planet-shattering boom and her head sank through the steel plating.

Iral's knee grew another joint as he knelt in front of her. 'I look forward to watching your progress, Ms Kuar. We shall be in touch.'

DON'T MISS ANOTHER BOOK!

I love keeping in touch with my readers, it's the second-best thing about being a writer (writing being the first best). Every fortnight (or thereabouts), I send out a newsletter with details about upcoming offers, new releases and extra special projects.

If you sign up for the mailing you'll receive exclusive behind-the-scenes extras, such as:

- free short stories
- deleted and alternate scenes from my books
- previews of upcoming books
- pancakes
- quizes
- and much, much more!

Scan the QR code or visit the link below to sign up.
belindacrawford.com/newsletter

ACKNOWLEDGEMENTS

Short Bits was inspired by my own self-doubts, or rather my response to those doubts. In the Introduction, I mention that the stories within were written as practice, and a large part of what I practised (and still practice) is defiance of my inner critic – that little voice that tries to convince all your words are rubbish – but I didn't do it alone.

Battling the inner critic is something that all writers, and indeed every artist, seems to go through. Demolishing it is neither easy nor pleasant and requires a certain amount of practice, not a little fortitude and outside assistance.

In my case, that outside assistance came from two sources, chief being industry veteran Dean Wesley Smith, through his many lectures and books. His advice is prosaic and not for the faint of heart, but always an inspiration and a reminder that great things can be accomplished simply by planting your bum in a chair, and your fingers on a keyboard.

Last but never least, is my ever-wonderful editor, Amanda J Spedding. I sent her *Short Bits* full of nerves and trepidation, worried that the collection was a steaming pile of yuck, and she turned around and simply said, "it works". I'm not sure she'll ever know just how much of relief her words were, but they took a great big weight off my shoulders.

Thanks Amanda, you're awesome.

ABOUT THE AUTHOR

Belinda Crawford is a science fiction author for readers who like their fiction action-packed, with diverse characters, butt-kicking heroines and complex worlds. The creator of The Hero Rebellion and the online serial, *Demons & Battleskirts*, her philosophy is to buck convention and "follow the awesome". Which pretty much means doing the unexpected in the most interesting way possible.

As a certified crazy horse person, when she's not wrangling six-legged dynamos on the page, she's wrangling four-legged powder-kegs in the paddock. Belinda brings that same certified craziness to her writing, with unexpected twists and enough wacky ideas to keep readers guessing.

You can keep in touch with Belinda, or just pick her brains about sci-fi via her website, Facebook or by sending her an email (she loves email).

www.belindacrawford.com
belinda@belindacrawford.com

Have news delivered straight to your inbox
via her mailing list. Sign up at:
belindacrawford.com/newsletter

www.ingramcontent.com/pod-product-compliance
Lightning Source LLC
Chambersburg PA
CBHW020534120726
47904CB00003B/1069